The Traveler and Other Short Stories

ISBN: 978-0-9988994-6-6

Printed in the USA by Steamy Trails Publishing

THE TRAVELER

AND OTHER SHORT STORIES

By

Anthony Arnold

A Word from the Author

Over the last twelve years, I've written 4 books about the history of being black. As this new year begins.

I'm going to do something a little different. A book of stories. With a little poetry thrown in. I hope that you enjoy it.

Anthony Arnold

The Kingpen

Foreword

In our lifetime, you rarely come across an individual whose perspective on life events of truth are presented in the form of poetry.

I am privileged and honored to have met one such individual. His name is Anthony Arnold, and he has been affectionately dubbed with the moniker of King Pen. Mr. Arnold demonstrates a passion for truth in his ink. When you read one of his poems you can feel the approval of the ancestors. It's as if they sit with him while he is scribing out the masterful works of their pain, our past, present, and future.

Anthony Arnold has created literary works of art that penetrate the heart and soul while stirring emotions that you never knew existed within yourself. As you read his poetry be prepared to be mesmerized in a journey of poetic justice.

From The Mind of Poetic
Van Meadows

Acknowledgments from My Readers

In one word: Real. I love reading the work of Anthony Arnold because he doesn't cloud the issues. He brings reality to the surface and makes you face it whether it's love, heartache, victory, or pain. His work is certainly a great testament to the times.

Ginger Galloway

Author Anthony's work hits your soul, and it makes you want to be a better person. He takes you on a journey to the past and you literally feel the impact of the injustices committed. His work carries you on a trip to the past while having a sprinkle of current events thrown in. His writing is impactful!

Sheila Moseley

Anthony Arnold's poetry should be heard with reverence. A thousand ancestors stand behind each line. While poetry often evokes and or creates an open heart, "KingPen" evokes and creates an open mind if you let it in. The story woven is of the threads that bind us to each other. Anthony Arnold brings the richness of history to bear in some of the most profoundly beautiful poetry of the 21st century. One day, when they speak of the Digital Renaissance in poetry, they will speak of him with reverence.

Sylvia L. Blalock,

CEO - Queendom Network

A Word from the Publisher

The following lines are written with a sincere desire to expose how proud I am of Author Anthony Arnold. It was four entire books ago that I met Anthony and he has been a house favorite from day one. Now, I know full well that a publisher should never show favorites, but Anthony has become family.

This is Anthony's fifth book with STP, and I couldn't be happier for him. His writing is blunt, instant gold and historic the moment he sets pen to paper.

Here's to many more...

Your Always Publisher,

- Katrina Gurl

CEO – Steamy Trails Publishing

Table of Contents

THE TRAVELER AND OTHER SHORT STORIES

The Traveler

I am the traveler. The last of a space-faring race who traveled the galaxy. We watched the development of species in thousands of worlds.

Unlike the watchers who refused to intervene, we would nudge a race if we thought it was needed. One planet that we did this to be the one you call...

Earth

I returned to earth during what you called the 60s. I was appalled by what I found. As I traveled the earth, the things that I saw were not what we intended for you. Instead of love and happiness, I saw war and pain. Unhappiness. Mistreatment of their fellow man. In the Americas, it was all backward. dark skinned were supposed to be the dominant race.

We had gotten this all wrong. This planet must be neutralized. Life had not evolved the way we intended.

Earth must be destroyed.

Wait. What is this? Could there be hope for this planet? Who is Martin Luther King Jr? Malcolm X, Mother Theresa, and Mahatma Gandhi? John and Robert Kennedy. Why would they care for these people? There's more. The students put their lives on the line to bring about equality.

And those who gave their lives as well.

A man of dark skin was elected as leader. They have brought themselves a reprieve. They have shown that despite differences, change can be achieved.

For now, I am the Traveler. I travel the universe.

Action Jackson

"Hello, my name is Thomas Jefferson Jackson. But you can call me Action. I'm a private eye out of Spokane Washington and I oversee anything and everything. I'm a veteran of the Air Force and now I do this to pass the time."

"It was a dreary day in Spokane, and I don't know why I even came into the office that Monday. It was snowing like no tomorrow, and I figured with the weather being bad, I could catch up on some paperwork. Boy, was I wrong!"

"My door opened a little after 9:00 a.m. and before I could say *'I'm closed'* this cool drink of water flowed into my office. Now mind you, I don't get tongue-tied often, but she was stunning. About 6'1, long flowing black hair, hazel eyes, and a body that could stop time and rewind! Her beauty took my breath away, but I finally was able to get four words out... "May I help you?"

"Yes," she said in a silky voice that had my mind going to other places. "Are you the one they call Action Jackson?"

"Yes, that's me." I felt a little sheepish at that nickname around her, but I shared that my gramps gave me that nickname when I was a baby because she said I was always ready for action. "Anyway, what can I do for you on this snowy day?"

"I need your help! This man is trying to kill me!"

She showed me a picture of an ordinary-looking guy. He didn't look like he could or would hurt anyone. "Who is he and why is he trying to kill you?"

"May I sit down?"

"Sure," clearing off a chair for her. As she sat and crossed those long legs, my imagination went wild...picturing her legs wrapped around me. It took all my strength to shake myself into realizing that lustful thoughts had caused me not to hear one word she said. "Excuse me what were you saying? And, please start again, with your permission, I'd like to record this." She just smiled as if she knew what I had been thinking.

"My name is Tal N. Sexy, and this man is my husband. I know you've heard of the Benson murder case in Tacoma."

"Wait, your husband is D.L. Sexy? The reported gangster? D.L Sexy ran everything from the numbers to prostitution and murder for hire, but had never been convicted. So, why does he want to kill you and what does this have to do with me?" I must admit I was puzzled.

"I can prove that he did kill James Benson, and he wants to tie up loose ends. This is where you come in! You were recommended to me by a friend from Tacoma's Police Department, Leland Byrd."

"Ah yes, the Byrd man! We had been through the wars together. Oh, ok I'm listening. What did Byrd tell you about me?"

"He said that you could be trusted and that you could keep me safe."

"What am I keeping you safe from?" I asked.

"My husband's people!" She said with a sigh. "His reach extends everywhere. Even to Spokane."

"I think you will be safe with me." She smiled and walked to the window and watched the snow fall into massive puddles of melted snow. I had my back turned to her when I heard her gasp for air as she fell to the floor.

I dived to the floor towards her as five more bullets entered the window. Her lifeless body lied right in front of me with shots center mass. She was dead before she hit the floor.

I was pissed! For one thing, I didn't like being shot at! And two, she came to me to keep her alive and I had already failed her right after I gave her my word. I don't like to fail.

I called Spokane PD and informed them of the shooting, and after being grilled for 5 hours, I called for someone to fix the window. From the looks of this case, I know I will be taking a trip to what will feel like the lion's den. I called Byrd... "Expect me, I'm coming to Tacoma!"

Tacoma

Action Jackson couldn't believe he was heading to Tacoma! He was shot at and witnessed a prospective client get gunned down in his office! Neither of which was he incredibly happy about. After calling his good friend at TPD, Leland Byrd.

From his connect in the med examiner's office, he was able to find out before hitting the road that the round that killed Mrs. Tal was a 7.62 sniper round. After a little research, the round was used in an M40 sniper rifle that was used by the Marine Corps.

Action thought, no wonder why the shots were never heard. Max effective range for that shell is eight hundred meters. Somebody wanted her dead with a minimal amount of fuss. But who?

Action had to look at all possibilities for Tal N. Sexy's shooter. Top of his list was now ex-husband D.L. Sexy. He had the most to lose if she went to the police. He was being looked at for the Benson murder and from what Tal told him in the office earlier, she also had evidence that proved D.L. did it. But what was that evidence and most importantly where was it?

It was late that evening when Action arrived in Tacoma, nicknamed the City of Destiny.
He called Leland to let him know where he'd be staying and he'd see him first thing the next day.

He didn't tell him that he'd be snooping around a little to see what he could find out on his own first though. Action checked into the Hotel Bostwick in downtown

Tacoma and got ready for what was going to be a long night.

After a slight nap and a little bit to eat, he got ready to go out. Action carries a Glock 19 for persuasion purposes; along with a small night vision camera. He also carries a few other things that he never mentions. He always says, 'a guy can't tell all of his secrets!'

He headed for the port area down near the waterfront. Figuring that he should be able to find out a few things there and also to let Mr. Sexy know that he at least wants to speak with him. The town was quiet, but that didn't surprise Action much. What surprised him was the long black limo that pulled up beside him. "Get in the car!" the gorilla said.

After being forced in the car, he realized that the gorilla had a twin. Action was shoved in the back seat between what looked like Tweedledum and Tweedledee. "Where are you taking me?" Jackson asked frantically. Tweedledum hit me with an elbow to the jaw, which I must admit rattled my cage a bit. Action looked at him and said, "If you do that again, I'll kill you where you sit!"

He proceeded to hit Action again when the other yelled, "The boss said he was not to be harmed!" Action gave a deep breath and decided to fall asleep. But not until crossing the Tacoma Narrows bridge. That bridge had always creeped Action out. Even though it's not the "Galloping Gertie" of the 1940's, he can still imagine that bridge peeling like an orange.... Gave him chills.

The limo pulled up in front of this large, elegant mansion. The aphasic twins let me out and told me to followed them. Taking in the scenery, immaculate rugs, and paintings of the well decorated house...Action had to remind himself that he was here by force and that this was a crime lord's house.

Tweedledum pushed him into the room with a sharp shove. Action realized it was time to give an example. "I told you if you touch me again, I would kill you where you stood."

Before he could move, he ripped his throat out and showed it to him. He gurgled once and fell to the floor, and bled all over a nice Persian rug worth more than Action made in a year.

"I apologize for that one's behavior," said a frail voice behind me. I turned to see a withered old man in a wheelchair coming into the room.

What was going on? Action thought to himself. Was this thee D.L. Sexy? Was the scourge of Tacoma? What had I gotten myself into?

Revelations

Action thought, 'I must admit that I was caught by surprised and that's hard to do. I had pictured him as a robust man; with an air of arrogance about him. But not this!

Barely able to roll the wheels of his chair, the frail man said, "Not what you expected? I can tell by the look on your face. I'm suffering from prostate cancer, not to mention all the women I laid up with unprotected; my condition is what it is. So, I heard that you wanted to see me. What can I do for you?"

Considering that Action had not spoken to anyone yet, he knew it had to be a leak in the PD. He would be sure to speak to Byrd about that when he seen him and with his current situation...if he would see him. "D.L., I hate to inform you, but your wife is dead. Of all the things that I expected him to do, this was not it." He started to cry. If you ordered the death of your wife, crying would be the last thing that you would do. I asked him, "Did you have Tal killed?"

"NO!" He said explosively. "I did not!"

After a moment in a voice that was so quiet, I could barely hear him ask, "How did she die?"

"She was killed with a sniper's rifle;" I told him still perplexed at his reaction.

"Sit down Mr. Jackson. Can I get you a drink?"

"Chivas regal one ice cube please." Gramps always taught me good manners! I sat down on a couch that was so plush that it almost swallowed me. D.L. rolled up to me and gave me my drink and told his minions, leave us! They complied reluctantly and closed the door behind them.

“Now ask me anything you want to know.” He said looking at me eye to eye.

This was the last thing that I expected. It seemed like I was working behind the eight ball. I needed to step up my game. I asked him directly; “did you have your wife killed?”

He said, “No, but I know who did! And it goes all the way up to the governor’s office.”

“So why did she tell me that she had evidence that could prove that you did it?”

“Because that’s what I wanted her to think. Jackson, I’m dying and she deserved more than me. Do you think I’m afraid of jail? I have 3 months left to live. Jail is the least of my worries.”

“But if you didn’t do it, why let her think that you did?”

“I have my reasons”.

“So, she went to her grave carrying an untruth about you and you don’t care? What kind of man are you?”

He looked at Action and said, “A dead one! I made sure that she could find the evidence that I had, and when she confronted me, I didn’t deny it, so she took it and left. She was supposed to be watched by my people to ensure nothing happened to her. That failure will be addressed."

I felt sorry for the person who had messed that up. He gave me a folder to read and said...

"Let me know what you think."

As I began to read, my heart began to rise into my throat. There were names and account numbers of important people in this. Including my friend Byrd. Now, what was I going to do? The one man that I trusted was in on it. And the one man that I thought was implicated in it, seemed to be the only one worth trusting.

Suddenly I heard a tinkle of glass, and as I went to shout, D.L. flew from his chair. He was killed by one bullet, center mass. The minions flew in and before I could tell them two of their heads exploded like ripe watermelons. We were under attack, but from whom and the bigger question was why?

Endgame

“Action!!! Action!!! I know that you’re in there! Come out and we can finish this!”

“Byrd??! What in hell?”

Why was he out there and better yet why was he shooting at me? He was one of my best friends or so I thought. We had been in the military together and even though I left first, he parlayed his experience into a job at Tacoma PD. I was the godfather to his son. What had I missed?

“Byrd! What’s going on? What are you doing?”

“I can’t let you dig into this. It’s my nest egg.”

“You killed Benson? Why?” I asked.

“Why? HAHAHAHA! He wouldn’t do what he was told anymore. He wanted to run the business and cut me out. I couldn’t let that happen. So, I killed him and made it look like sexy did it. I knew he was dying and even if he did get convicted, he wouldn’t have lived long enough to do any time anyway! His wife was a nice piece too. We saw each other twice a week. She wanted to make sure that none of the stuff with Sexy would fall on her. She didn’t know that she was going to go down too. She must have learned something cause the next thing I know; she is running to you…so she had to be eliminated!”

“Damn!” Action remembered that Byrd had sniper training when we were in the military. Lucky for me, he's is too close to me to use that thing on me! At least that's in my in my favor.

"Come on out, I promise to kill you quick," Byrd yells!

Action could see which way this is going to go. He was going to have to keep him talking and use the darkness as an equalizer in this standoff. There still was too much light to use the night vision camera, so the old Mark-one eyeballs will have to do. The first order of business is to get out of this death trap.

He was able to make my way to a side door and get out of it. Looks like it was time to use the extra goodies he brought with him. He snuck up behind one of Byrd's hired goons and took out a stainless-steel garrote. By the time this poor sap knew anything he was decapitated with his head hanging by a few muscles. This was going to be a warning for everyone involve, which was what he wanted.

After disposing a couple more of the hired help, he was able to make his way where Byrd was. He wasn't happy that they couldn't find him. He shot one of them point blank and told the others to find me or else. I stayed hidden and watched the person who I thought was my friend. The more I watched, the more I didn't recognize him. This needed to be over with. Now!

"You looking for me," Action said softly.

Byrd turned around and smiled. "I wondered how long it would take you to find me. You always were a good tracker".

"Yeah, yeah enough with the flowery crap. All I want to know is why. What happened to you?" he growled.

"What happened to me? I found an opportunity and I took it. You would have done the same thing.

Action sighed, "This isn't about me. You have a wife and kids. What about them?"

Byrd raged, "She left me and took the kids six months ago. You haven't even bothered to check-in. I caught Benson swindling money from a government account and instead of arresting him, I made myself his partner. It was going well until he decided to cut me out. So, I killed him and blamed it all on D.L. Sexy. How was I to know that he had a snitch in the office?"

"You know that I can't let you get away with this." Smiling Byrd said. "Ah come on friend. I'll bring you in, and get you some good money."

Action shook his head, "Nah I'm good." Byrd started to walk away and said,

"I guess you must die too." He spun and pulled out a pistol. Action dropped to one knee and pulled his Glock! We both fired at the same time.... BLAM!!!

Epilogue Six Months Later

Sitting on the beach, in Tampa Florida recuperating and trying to figure out what had gone wrong with Byrd. He had a respectable job, and a family. Heck, he had all the things I wanted but never got, Action thought to himself. He loved being a PI but getting shot at over and over gets old. Good thing Byrd missed and only him in the shoulder. And, though Action didn't want it to come to this, he ended up giving Byrd a third eye. Action gave the info that Sexy gave him to the FBI and let them manage it. I was done for a while; with a much-needed vacation.

Action walked back to the hotel and noticed a package at door. This was strange because no one knew where he was. Or so he thought. It seemed to be legit, so he took it into the room and opened it. Inside was a letter with a picture and a half million in cash. Action counted that cash three times just to make sure.

The letter stated:

Mr. Jackson,

I hope this letter finds you in good health and in case you are wondering, it is I, D.L Sexy. My wife Tan says hi also. Sorry, that we put you through that little charade, but we knew that Byrd was looking to kill us, so we had doubles.

I'm glad that you are alive, and you don't have to worry about the bills, they have been taken care of. The two of us have retired and are no longer in the States. We hope that this will compensate you for your time.

Be well,

D.L. and Tal N. Sexy

Action looked again at the money and smiled.
Although he had one question for him.

Action always wanted to know what D.L. stood for.

THE END???

The Return of Action Jackson

It had been a year since the D.L. Sexy's case. Action retreated to his home in the country to decide what he wanted to do next. Money wasn't an issue; especially with what Sexy gave him. Action thought he was getting too old for this, but he still could kick ass with the best of them. Although recovery time was getting longer and longer, it was just time for Action to become plain old TJ or so he thought.

1 year later

The year had gone by quickly and Action had regained strength in his shoulder. For 54 he felt good. There was a knock at the door that interrupted him congratulating himself in the mirror. He walked towards the door thinking; who in the hell is this? He most definitely wasn't expecting anyone. "May I help you!"

"Yes, we are looking for the man named Action Jackson...would you happen to be him?"

The hairs stood up on the back of his neck, as these two didn't look like the local Seventh-day Adventists. "No, I'm sorry, you have the wrong house. He used to live here, but he moved."

"Sorry to have disturbed you, sir."

Hansel and Gretel walked back to the longest black limo Action had ever seen. Well, at least he thought they looked like Hansel and Gretel. One of them was a woman...at least she minimally looked like a woman.

After the interruption, Action walked to the garden to pruning his flowers and mind his own business. Just as he pushed back the first row to prune, that proved to be a most fatal mistake.

Act II

Action awoke to the smell of smoke in the early morning. It was coming from his own house! Hansel and Gretel must of knew they were being lied to straight to their faces.

Action jumped up and pulled something on and grabbed his war bag out of the closet.
He made it out of the house just before the roof collapsed. He then overheard firefighters in the distance saying no one could have lived through that inferno.

Hearing that, immediately gave Action an idea. If people thought he was dead, he could then figure out what this is all about. It was a damn shame about the house. He had just got it the way he wanted it. 'Oh well,' he thought, as he made it back through the forest to his backup area. Just like Batman...he too had a bat cave.

Act III

Soon as he got in safe, he called Katrina Gurl, his banker. Action told her what was going on and that he'd be laying low for a while, but would still need access to funds and needed to get something out of a safety deposit box. She told me to meet her at the bank's back door at 9 PM.

Action got there at 9:00 sharp and saw Katrina's car parked at the bank. As he walked up, he thought he heard a noise, so he dropped to the ground just as a bullet passed over where he was standing. There were more shots fired in his direction.

Although they weren't shooting directly at him, he made his way around the back side of that same black limo that was in his front yard yesterday. It was time to get some answers for this charade.

"DON'T MOVE!" Action yelled. Hansel spun around and I shot him in the kneecap. He screamed! "You shot me in the knee!"

"And for good measure..." BLAM! Hansel got shot in the other knee! "And now you have a matching set!" As Action took Hansel's gun, he asked him, "Where is that sister of yours, and why are the two of you trying to kill me?"

"I'm over here," she said, as she walked through the clearing holding Katrina in front of her.

"Well, isn't this a fine kettle of fish?"

Act IV

Action positioned himself so he could see Hansel and Gretel. He could tell Katrina was pissed. Not only was she a good banker, but she was also the local fashion plate too. Action could see from the oil stains that her dress was ruined. He knew that was going to hurt the old pocketbook. “Let her go she has nothing to do with this.” He yelled to Gretel!

“No, I don’t think so. I think I will kill her in front of you before I kill you slowly.”

She stared at me while she licked the side of Katrina’s face. Action could see that this chick is seriously unhinged. Meanwhile Hansel is on the ground crying.

“He shot me, he shot me.”

“SHUT UP YOU FOOL!” She snapped off a shot which stopped his whining. Permanently. One shot. Center mass. And Action immediately recognized that shooting.

“It was you. It was you not Byrd.”

“No, it was both of us. I was always better at long range than he was. I was the one who shot that bitch in your office.”

That just brought the old anger back to Action. This bitch was going down and going down hard. All the while our little te-a-te was going on; Katrina was giving me little hints that she wanted this to be over. It was time to end this.

"So how did you like screwing your brother? You both look like you both couldn't get any from anyone else. You are a poor excuse for a woman! Look at your flat-chest and no ass at all. I know ironing boards with more curves." That last comment raged Gretel.

Katrina screamed and stepped on Gretel's foot with those 4-inch heels and fell. Action hit Gretel's forehead with a double tap from the Glock. She fell with a surprised look on her face. "Yes, I too can shoot quite well too!" He then walked over to help Katrina up off the ground when she yelled "WATCH OUT!!"

Action spun and felt an impact on his left shoulder...again! Oops! He shot one round that caught Gretel in her open mouth and blew out the back of her head. He walked over and emptied the clip. He wanted to make sure she was dead.

Epilogue

Katrina was able to get all my money from the bank. Action Jackson was laid to rest. Since there was no body from the fire, just an empty grave was all that was left.

He moved to Florida and took a whole new identity and he live in a nice house where he tended to his garden. His shoulder healed and he kept in shape.

Action was grocery shopping one day when this police officer walked up to him and said, "Are you, Action Jackson?"

"I'm sorry. You have me mistaken for someone else. It's nice to meet you, but my name is Anthony Arnold!"

Black Wall Street (a fictional account)

May 31, 1921. That date will always remain etched into my mind and soul. You see, that was the date that everything began to change. That everything was no longer the way it was. That we were no longer what we had been. Our own.

The beginning...

My name is James Johnson, and I own a little store in Greenwood, a suburb of Tulsa in Oklahoma. A man named O.W. Gurley purchased land in 1906 with the express purpose of selling land to colored folk. This was unheard of at the time. A lot of prominent Black people lived in the area. I came west from New York looking to start a new life. To forget her. She who had broken my heart.

I purchased a store with the money that I brought with me and began to etch out an honest living. I was even able to love again. I married sweet Jessica, a local girl and even though we were not able to have children, we adopted a child that had been left on the church steps. Our shop grew along with everything in the area. Prosperity was good. There were more airplanes owned by our people than by the whole state of Oklahoma Everything was going well...or so we thought.

The elevator...

May 30, 1921. A lovely day in Greenwood. Children playing, a band playing in the park. Business was good. What we didn't know was that around the corner at the Drexel building, things were playing out in a way that would change our way of life forever.

Dick Rowland, an elevator attendant and Sarah Page, a worker; according to whom you talked to were dating or not. No one knows what happed in that elevator, but we do know that the woman claimed rape, and he was arrested. It all went downhill from there. Arrested and put in jail, we were all in fear for his life. None of us thought that we would ever see him again.

The riots...

May 31, 1921. I opened my shop as I normally did. Spoke to some of the other shopkeepers and waited for Jessica to come down to the shop with little James like she always did. There was a buzz in the air about the arrested man sitting in jail. There had been a mob of white folks down at the jail all night. So far nothing has happened.

So far...

I was in the shop talking with Jessica when there was a big fuss outside. I walked out to see what was wrong and seen a group of Black people arguing about the headlines in the paper. The Tulsa Tribune put out the afternoon edition at about 3. I wouldn't use that waste of a rag to wipe a bear's butt. But others swore by it. The headline *said 'Negro Nabbed for Attacking White Girl in the Elevator.'* There was an ill wind blowing and I needed to get my family away. I told Jessica to take little James home and go to her family's house, that way they would be safe. I boarded up the store and waited.

7:34 pm

I'm here at the jail with some other Black people trying to save this boy's life. The sheriff is determined there will be no lynching. The pawn shop owners opened their stores to the crowd. Now it's seven hundred angry whites to thirty blacks and the sheriff and his crew. They were determined that he would die, and we were determined that he wasn't.
More blacks and more whites came to the courthouse. All were armed. Our being there was being taken as a "negro uprising." We were told to surrender our guns. Of course, we said no. A shot was fired, no one knows by who.

It has begun.

June 1, 1921, 01:00 a.m. We are in a fight for sure. Whites shooting innocent folks and burning shops. The National Guard is here but has been no help. Over on Archer Street buildings are burning. Mobs would not let the fire department put the fires out, so the Black-owned businesses burned...including mine.

Black people began to leave in a mass exodus to try and save themselves and their families. The mob fired on them as they wished. People were killed just trying to live. We tried to give as well as we got, but there were just too many. We could only do what we could to survive.

Daybreak...

It arrived at the sound of a lonely whistle. And all hell broke loose. Fires had been burning since last night. None were allowed to be put out. Now with the sunrise, a new threat arose.

Airplanes.

Biplanes left over from war training now became the seeds of our destruction. Homemade bombs and gunfire rained down upon us. There was nowhere to run. Nowhere to hide. Black and whites were killed or injured. It didn't matter. Jealousy from those that coveted what we had took the opportunity to loot, burn and destroy.
I was able to make it to Jessica's family. The car was packed, and we all left. There was nothing left for us here...nothing for any of us.

Epilogue

I finally came back to Greenwood for the first time. Little James said it was time to return and bury all the feelings that we had had over the years. There was also one other reason to come back. To lay Jessica to rest in the town of her birth.

As we travel along Archer and Greenwood, some of the buildings remain. But not many. There are plaques lying on the sidewalks where some of the buildings once stood. Tears came to my eyes to see the plaque where my store one stood. I was glad that Jessica was not here to see this. It would have broken her heart.

They said that only thirty-six people lost their lives, but others said around 300 were killed. Picked up and thrown on flatbed trucks, buried in unmarked graves. Over 1200+ buildings and businesses were burned, looted, or both. About 1.8 million in damages.

The sheriff was charged with not doing his job but never served any time. Rowland stayed safe in jail and was taken out of town in secrecy. The charges were dropped, and he never returned to Tulsa.

It's time to go home now, I made my home elsewhere, but this was a chapter in my life that I had to close. And now it's done. May those that died here rest in peace?

The End

[***Thanks to Greenwood historian Lee Alford for background information for this piece.***]

Do We Understand the Assignment?

One question needs to be asked.

Simple and plain

For us as a people

For all generations

Do we understand the assignment?

For us to survive

Separation cannot be prevalent.

Young and old

We Must help one another.

Divide and conquer cannot be overwhelming.

Black men support our women.

Black women support our men.

Black people support us.

We will only win together.

The children are the future.

Teach them the ways of our ancestors.

Teach them our history!

And if you don't know

Become learned yourself.

Those of us that try to teach.

That tries to inform.

We are slowly leaving this earth.

Those that follow ask the question.

Tunaelewa kazi

Do we understand the assignment?

Escape - A Story of Perseverance

In the future...

I listened as I heard the slave hunters go by. "I know I saw that nigger come through here." There is no way that he could have come through here, look at that thicket, he would have to be a fool to go that way. Even the dogs won't go that way. Let's look elsewhere. As they went away from my hiding place, I felt relieved. I removed myself from the thicket and dabbed mud on my wounds. There was no time to rest. I had to keep moving. My life depended on it. I thought about my condition as I moved deeper into the forest towards freedom.

The beginning

It began as I was captured in my homeland and was stolen away to this strange land across the big pond. I was taken as I carried water from the river to my village. That jug was the last thing that I will ever remember from my family and my home. My cries were silenced by a blow from a very pale man. A bright light then darkness became my world.

I awakened chained to another child in the bottom of something, I knew not what. There was moaning and crying all around me. The smell of vomit and feces ran rampant here. I called out to anyone, anyone that could help me. My voice was drowned out, for I was only a child. I made a promise that one day my voice would someday be heard.

Many cycles passed, before I learned that what I was on had been a large ship. They took us up on the top to rinse the feces and vomit off us and to let us get sunlight. Many of us died and were thrown overboard. The waters ran red with their blood. I prayed to my god, why had he forsaken me? But I received no answer. Storms followed us as we traveled across the great water. Two ships disappeared never to be seen again. Again, I prayed to my god, but I had received my answer. He had taken those two ships and allowed me to live.

Our journey finally ended in a strange land. We were washed and scrubbed with water from the great pond. The water burned as it got into the wounds from the chains and shackles. We were given clothes that scraped the skin and opened the sores that had scabbed over. Chained to each other, we were led to a pen where we were grouped like cattle by age and sex.

We were then taken to another pen where were groped and sold to the pale men and women. I was taken along with a group of 5 other males and 3 other females. We were half marched, and half dragged behind a wagon to what was to be my place of existence for the next 5 years. Until I decided that I would gain my freedom. That I would be a free man. That I would ... ESCAPE!!!

Escape-Desperation

It has been a year since I was brought here against my will. From my group of people, there was only me and a young girl left. The master takes her to his room every night and her screams can be heard all over the farm. Yet no one does anything about it. It is accepted. The screams remind me of the screams in my village. I cannot attend this, but my time will come. Yes, it will come.

Working on the farm, my hands are rough and hard. I am now a muscled man, yet I am still a child. I have tasted the overseer lash and have the scars to match. As I pick this cotton and tobacco, I let my mind wander. How can I get away from this place? I am a free man, yet I am corralled like an animal. I cannot live like this. I must leave...tonight!

Midnight...

I slipped out of the shed that I lived in, no existed in. As I moved into the bushes into the woods, I could sense freedom in my grasp. I traveled throughout the night resting during the day. I was sure that I was being followed, but I never saw anyone, so I pressed on.

After 5 cycles of the sun, I was sure that I had gotten away from the plantation and the hated life that I had been forced into. Not that I just needed to keep going. To a new life. To freedom. I let my eyes close as I tried to rest another day.

I awoke to barking dogs and screaming men. We got him; we got the nigger. Roughly dragged by my feet with my hands bound, I was dragged to a horse and put on its back. I was taken to a tree where there was a noose hanging down. It dawned on me that I was to be hanged. I fought with all my being, but there were too many. I was struck on the head by one of their firesticks. Confused, I was held up while the rope was put around my neck.

As my vision cleared, I saw the overseer looking at me with a smile on his face. This will teach you to run away, won't it? He struck the animal, who took off running. I felt the pressure around my neck as I began to swing from the rope I wondered. Had I come so far just to die this way? Swinging from the end of a rope...?

Escape - Resurrection

Where am I?

Am I dead? Have I crossed over to the land of my ancestors? The last thing I remember is the pressure around my neck as the rope tightened. I gasped as the air could no longer reach my chest. I saw my family as consciousness seeped away from my mind. A shock of pain and then...

My eyes fluttered open, yet I could not see. I was in total darkness all around. I dared not call out, as I did not know where I was. A groan escaped my lips as I tried to move around. Ah, you're awake. We wondered if we had reached you in time. Relax and rest. Your throat is bruised, and you won't be able to talk for a while. Here is some cool water. Drink slowly and rest. It hurt to swallow, but I did as the person said. Slowly I felt sleep overcome me. I welcomed it with open arms.

I awoke again to see a stern woman sitting next to me. "Who are you? Where am I?" I said in a rough voice. I rubbed my throat and felt the scar of the rope around my neck. The woman watched as I rubbed the scar around my neck. She finally said "That is a reminder of how close you came to death. Remember it well!" she said, as she walked out of the room.

I did not see the woman for a couple of days while I gathered my strength. My voice had become raspy, and I was told that it would never change. She handed me a scarf and said wear this if you wish for people not to stare. I looked around and asked where am I?

"You are at a station on the Underground Railroad. We help slaves to escape." At the look on my face, she smiled and said "There is no train, but there is a route."

"Who are you," I asked as she turned left to leave the room.

She turned and with a solemn look said, "I am Harriet Tubman, and I am your best hope of survival".

Escape-Redemption

"I am Harriet Tubman and I am your best hope of survival." Her eyes pierced into mine as she stared into my face. I felt my soul open as she spoke to me, but I never heard her words. All I could focus on were her eyes, Burning, burning, and burning.

I stayed with Miss Tubman and the railroad for a week; traveling by night and hiding by day. There were even the pale ones who helped us by getting us food and clothing. I felt that I could not stay with them for much longer. I needed to be on my own. I needed to be free. I told Miss Tubman of my wish and even though she did not agree with me, she wished me well. So, with a small package of clothing and food, I gave my farewell and moved off into the forest.

After the company the past week, I never felt more alone. I heard voices everywhere I went. Sleep was hard to come by. I kept seeing the rope going around my neck and the pressure as it tightened. I always came awake as I fell off the animal as the rope tightened. Dogs I heard barking, men I heard yelling in the distance. My mind was not my own anymore.

Mungu ila mimi. God save me.

I awoke as a cool breeze blew across my body. I was covered with sweat. I reached up and felt the scar around my neck. Yes, this has been no dream. It had all been real. I needed to find a cover. I had been lying out in the open, yet I had not been discovered. The gods had indeed been looking over me. I went to find shelter, to hide until the safety of the night.

Epilogue

I made it to the north after two more months. I was taken in by a couple and taught to be a blacksmith, where I still work to this day. My dream of being a free man became a reality. I sometimes wonder what became of those who journeyed from the homeland with me. Were they as lucky as I was, or did they die a shameful death in a land that was not their own?

Harriett Tubman and the Underground Railroad were freed by some estimates of 100,000 slaves over the period of the railroad. Even though this is a fictional account, who is to say that it didn't happen?

The End

My Ancestors Pain

Nisaidie

Nisaidie

My ancestors, please

Nisaidie*

What have I done?

This pain seeps into my soul

Please

Nisaidie

I am no one important.

Just a simple farmer

Yet I was taken, not stolen.

Put in a place.

That I know not where.

This pale man beats me.

Yelling words, I cannot understand.

This thing rips my skin.

Sheds my lifeblood.

I pray now for relief.

For life

Please my gods

Nisaidie

Nisaidie

*Help me

It Burns

The fire within
My ancestors speak to me.
Stoking the fire

That much more

The lives lost.
The cities were destroyed.
How can this be?
Why was it allowed?

What did we do?

Tulsa, Rosewood
Seattle, Philadelphia
The town burned or bombed.
The common denominator

Black people or towns are gone.

Sundown towns
Don't let the sun go down on you.
A book to tell you safe places to go.
The Green Book

We traveled anyway.

My fire burns to tell the stories.
To share the hurt, the pain
To show the heart, the determination
Apple with

A fire that burns within.

The Journey

She waited until there was no moon.

She wanted no light to shine.
The darker the better
She wasn't worried about the way.

The route was in her head.

She had told them.
Meet me by the hanging tree at 2.
Take only what you can carry.
If you fall behind

You will be on your own.

There were only five of them.
No more, no less
Superstitious maybe
Careful definitely

Travel by night
Rest by day
Nothing is left behind.
To leave a trail

To give a clue

10 to 20 miles they traveled.
Helped by others.
To make it to safety
To Freedom

Her load was delivered.

She takes time to rest.
Soon she will head back.
To take others to freedom

To take the journey

The Phone Call

It was a voice that he never thought he would hear again. And a call he never thought he would receive. As he sat there in the restaurant where he agreed to meet her, he wondered how his life had come to this point.

Theirs was a tumultuous relationship, two strong-willed individuals neither wanting to give an inch. Neither at home nor at work. They fought hard and loved even harder. Their love burned as hot as the sun and flamed out like a supernova. In the end, they both left the relationship, broken, scared and afraid to love or trust again.

It had been a hard 10 years for him. He had not been able to commit to anyone, mainly because he still loved her. And, from what he heard through the grapevine she had not done too well either. Married and divorced twice. Damn, as he shook his head, twice!

Good, he thought if I'm miserable she should be too. Stop! That's one of the reasons that you are in the position you're in, being a smart ass.

Someone caught his eye and he saw her before she saw him. He watched her as she strolled up the street. Hair and makeup were exquisite and clothing well matched. He found himself smiling, yeah that's my baby. He banished that thought as soon as it came to his head. She no longer belonged to him; he was just someone from the past.

She finally spotted him sitting at the table and made her way to him. He stood and pulled out a chair for her. “Thank you,” she said as she kissed him on his cheek. She took her time looking him over. Hmmm she thought, he still looks and smells good. What in the hell was I thinking?

He felt her gaze, but he didn’t know what to say or do. Well, bring it out in the open, I guess. “Why did you leave?”

She had to think for a moment. Why did she leave? She didn’t know. He had taken good care of her. Was she restless? She knows why. But while looking into his eyes, she knew he expected an answer.

“I don’t know why I left. I woke up one morning and I felt something was missing. I know that you loved me but somehow that wasn’t enough, I had to have more. So, I left. That’s one of the reasons why I called you. There are some things that I need to say to you, because I may not be able to later.” “What do you mean you may not be able to later? What is this, some kind of confession to make you feel better? I don’t need your pity. I did the best I could for you. I gave you everything you ever wanted. Not what you needed, WANTED! It took me ten long, long years to get over you, and now you just want to waltz back into my life as if nothing happened. Not only no, but HELL NO!”

As he went to get up, he heard this tiny voice say something that stopped him dead in his tracks.

“I have AIDS.”

“You what”? He couldn’t believe what he had heard. He slowly sat back down and looked at her. “How? When? Where? Am I infected too”? His head started to spin. He couldn’t believe what she just said. She didn’t look sick. Was this just a sick joke?

“I am serious about this. And before you ask no you are not infected. My second husband gave it to me. He was a down-low brother, and I didn’t know until he got sick. He just passed 6 months ago. That’s why I called you. I know I’m dying, and I don’t want to die alone. I wanted to spend my final days with you to try and make up for the time that I hurt you. Please say yes.”

He was torn as to what to do; she had come back into his life only to leave him again. He knew that he would say yes. He still loved her, and he always would so he said the only thing he could say…“YES!”

2 years later….

They had lived a full life. They traveled the world. They did everything that they could do. Once again, their love burned with an unmatched passion. But they both knew that the end would come, and preparations were made and finalized. When the end came it came with a viciousness that neither one of them expected.

One morning she became ill, and he rushed her to the ER. As they ran tests, the doctor came and said she may not make it till morning. “Ok, he said I’m taking her home.”

He went into the room and looked at her with tears in his eyes. She looked at him and said "I know. Can we go home?" He tenderly took her in his arms and carried her in his arms and drove her home.

He held her in his arms for the rest of that night. They talked when she could, but he let her rest. She had one last request. She wanted him to take her to the sunroom so she could see the Sunrise?

They sat together in the big chair facing the east. The sun rose and it was the best sunrise either of them had ever seen. She said, "Oh my," then she was gone. He held her tightly as the sun continued to rise, and at that moment a white dove was silhouetted in the sky. He knew then that everything would be all right.

Her ashes were spread over the ocean as she wished, and the money that she left was donated in her name for AIDS research. He knew he would always love her. For always.

Wayne Stewart- The University Murders

1:00 am

Laura Jackson cursed her luck for the tenth time. Walking home on University Blvd. after losing her wallet. Or having it stolen, she thought. I should have been in my room studying. But I needed to get out of the dorm, or I was going to go stir-crazy. The bad thing about all of this was she couldn't get a ride back to the dorm either. So, on foot, she would go. She figured the walk would do her some good. She forgot she was wearing heels until the one on the right foot snapped and broke.

Damn! She thought as she pulled off her shoes. That was my favorite pair of shoes. That was her last conscious thought as she was struck from behind.

He struck her repeatedly until she was unrecognizable. He dragged her into an alley, pulled off his coveralls, and left all of it next to her. A slight smile registered on his face as he looked into the rear-view mirror while he drove off.

Present day

My name is Wayne Stewart. I'm a private investigator working out of Riverside California. I was a 25-year veteran of the Riverside PD before I went into business for myself. I wasn't doing badly as a PI. The connections I made while I was on the police force came in right handy. Right now, business is slow, so it gave me some time to catch up on my paperwork. The only thing I hate. Maybe one day I'll get a secretary. The ringing of the phone snapped me out of my reveille.

"This is Wayne, how can I help you?" "Wayne, this is Chief Smith down at the PD". "Hi Chief, what can I do for you." I was wondering if you could come down, so we could have a chat. Off the record." That perked my senses up. Real quick. Something must be going on if the Chief wants to talk off the record. "Ok Chief, when do you want to get together?" "Would tomorrow at 9 am be ok?" "Sure, I don't have anything going on." "Ok I'll see you then and Wayne don't say anything to anyone about our conversation." "Ok Chief, see you in the am." "Thanks Wayne, see you tomorrow. Bye."

I hung up the phone and sat back in my chair. I wondered what was going on. I hadn't heard of anything, not even from my friends on the force. I turned back to my paperwork. I got the feeling that I wouldn't be able to finish it for quite some time.

Chapter 2 Wayne Stewart - The University Murders

I got down to headquarters at 8:45 the next morning. I figured that I didn't want to be late for this; whatever it was. As I walked in, I said hi to some of the guys that I knew that were still on the force and shot the crap with them for a bit. I glanced at my watch; it was 5 till. I said my goodbyes and ran to the chief's office. Just as I got there, his secretary said, go on in Wayne. He's expecting you. I walked in and came to a complete stop and to say I was shocked was an understatement!

In the office next to the chief, was the under chief, Chief Jackson, the District Attorney Evelyn Gonzalez, and someone whose name I didn't catch. But I was willing to bet he was from one of the alphabet agencies. "Sorry I'm late chief." He waved me off and said...

"You're not late, we got here early. Now that we are all here, Marolyn see that we are not disturbed for anything or anyone. Including the mayor."

"Yes, sir," Marolyn said as she closed the door.

"Now that we are all here, we can bring Wayne up to date."

The guy in the suit said, "I'm raising my objection to this once again. We don't need a private investigator for this. We can bring him in on our own!"

The under chief turned at him and said, "If that was true, I wouldn't have to bury my little girl."

“Wait hold up...would someone tell me what is going on here?!!” Mr. Suit as I called him began to speak.

“About a year and a half ago, a young girl was walking home from a late shift at a local restaurant. She never made it home. Her parents called the local police after she didn’t show up at home and missed her next work shift. A search group was formed and after 24 hours her body was found in a shallow grave. She had been beaten with a blunt object until she was unrecognizable.

“There were no subjects and from the interviews that were conducted and she had no enemies. The dogs found a bloody jumpsuit close to the site, but there wasn’t a match to any known criminals. About a month later, another girl was taken and killed the same way. Beaten beyond recognition. No subjects were ever found. After 2 more killings, we were called in. but our profilers couldn’t give us a solid profile. All they could tell us was he hated young women and he had a great amount of rage.”

I asked Mr. Suit, “Were the victims close to each other in age? Did they resemble each other at all? Were any of them prostitutes?”

At that, the under chief bristled. Before the under chief could say anything, Mr. Suit said “No, none were prostitutes. 2 were college students, one was a waitress, and the other was a mom coming from a night with the girls. She was the only one that was different from the others. She was found on the steps to her house, plus she was older. The other women were in their 20s, she was in her mid-30s.”

"You can disregard her I said. She was killed as a decoy, to throw you off the trail. The victims are going to be in the mid-20 range. They will be women who are either coming home from work or coming home from a night out.

"Where did the first killings take place?"

"Northern California, why?"

Now he has moved to Southern California. So, I wonder why. Could it be that he's coming home? There must be a reason why. We just have to figure out why. I looked at the under chief and said,

"I'm sorry for your loss." He looked at me with a startled look and said,

"How did you know?"

"You bristled when I asked if any of the victims were prostitutes. Plus, you never looked up while the FBI was talking."

Mr. Suit just looked at me with a stone-cold look, but he said nothing.

"Miss Gonzalez, what is your part in this?"

"If you decide to help us, I will be your contact. Everything you do will be approved by me."

"Wait right there. That's where you're wrong. If I do this, I do it my way or not at all. I'm not a member of the police force anymore. Remember you came to me. It's either my way or the highway. I'm sure the FBI can continue to do their usual wonderful job."

I got up to leave and the chief said, “Wayne, give us a minute!”

I walked out the door and hobnobbed with Marolyn, whom I used to have a big crush on. Her phone buzzed after about 5 minutes, and she just pointed at the chief's door. I walked in and it looked like there had been a knock down drag out argument. The only two happy faces were the chief and under chief. The DA looked like she had sucked on a lemon and Mr. Suit still had that stone-cold look on his face. I made a note to keep an eye on him.

The chief said “Okay Wayne it’s your show. If you need anything, DA Gonzalez will funnel your requests. The under chief will help with manpower if you need it. The FBI will stay in the background until needed.”

“Ok, the first thing I need is any information that any of you have on the murders, if any of the victim’s crossed paths with each other. We got to hope that he won’t kill before we can formulate some type of plan.” We weren’t going to be that lucky.

Chapter 3 - Downtown Riverside

She came out of the club with her friends still flushed with excitement. "Girl, did you see him?" Sara said to her friends. "He was just too, too fine."

"Yeah, and too, too young for you."

"He wasn't that young. Besides, I need to get my groove on."

"Child, you need to go home and put your tired behind to bed."

"Yeah, I know. Got to make that paper in the morning." Sara kissed her friend on the cheek and said that she would see her at work.

"You know you can stay with me. It isn't like you don't have clothes over there."

Sara thought about it for a minute but said, "Naw, I'm going to go home. Need to feed my cat."

"Ok then see you at work."

"You too", Sara said over her shoulder. Those were the last words Sara said to anyone again.

I got a call at 5:00 a.m. the next day from the under chief. "Wayne, can we see you downtown on the campus of the university?"

"Where," I asked.

"The University Blvd. entrance. You can't miss it."

"Okay, I'll be right there." I put my coffee pot on and jumped into the shower. As I got dressed, I thought, he didn't give us long to think about this. If this continues at this pace, we may be in a world of hurt. I grabbed my coffee and headed out.

The under chief was right, I couldn't miss it. The area was lit up like a sports stadium. The gang was all there. They all looked like they had rolled out of bed. Unkempt. Except one. Mr. Suit looked as if he had spent some time in the mirror. Interesting. He started to walk toward me. I waved him off as I went to talk to the chief and the DA.

"What happened?" DA Gonzalez said.

"One of the university police officers was doing building checks when he saw something strange in the bushes. He discovered her body in the position she's in now. He's over there talking to Officer Patterson." I walked over to where the two officers were talking. As I got closer the university officer looked familiar. Officer Patterson mind if I ask this officer a couple of questions?

"Hi Wayne, no go ahead."

I looked at the officer and said, "your name is?

"Arnold. Anthony Arnold. How can I help you?" Well Officer Arnold, can you tell me what you found. He stood there for a minute before he began to speak.

"I was doing my walk around here at the building. I saw that some of the shrubs had been knocked down. Some of the students like to take them. As I looked over at the shrubs, I saw what looked to be a woman's leg. As I looked closer, I saw her lying in the bushes.

She had ligature marks around her neck and wrists. She had been beaten beyond recognition."

"Thank you, Officer Arnold, if you think of anything else, please give me a call." As I gave him one of my cards, we both looked at each other. I said, "Do I know you from somewhere?"

He said "I don't think so. I'll call you if I remember anything."

Look at them. They have no clue what they are doing. I've left them enough clues. It's time for me to step it up just a little bit, come on Puppy, let's go home. I have a treat for you.

Chapter 4

He sat in his home away from home. The place where he could be himself, not the suited FBI agent that he has to be every day. He hated that person, but he was a needed persona. He planned to get rid of him after he finished this. He wanted, no he needed to finish this quickly. That PI. It looked like he didn't play any games, and he didn't want to be too cocky. He looked at his dossier on Stewart.

On paper, he didn't look like much. But he felt a chill when he looked into his eyes. He could be dangerous. If necessary, he would take him out. But he would save him for last. He looked over at was left of the puppy that he took on the walk. Sorry old chum.

No witnesses. As he turned away, his eyes fell on his next victim. DA Gonzalez. This should shake them up quite a bit. As he walked out of the door, he thought about Michael Keaton in Batman. I got to go to work.

Evelyn Gonzalez did as she did every night. She walked out of the gym in Moreno valley refreshed. Anyone that knew her knew she was a gym rat. It was her way of taking out her frustrations from the job. She won the DA's job by a narrow fifty votes. The incumbent played dirty and brought the fact that she was a lesbian into the campaign.

Some people said they didn't want a LGBTQ to represent them. But she overcame that and won the election. Since she got in, she proved that she knew what she was doing. She didn't give the tough cases to the assistants; she took them herself. Her conviction rate was a sparkling 98 percent. But none of that mattered now. All that mattered was a hot shower, and maybe some strawberry ice cream.

She was startled out of her daydream by Suit's voice. "Hey Gonzalez, hold up. Geez where's the fire?" As Suit walked up to her, he looked her up and down.

"Damn he thought, all of that going to waste." He knew she was gay from her dossier. He shook that out of his head and put his stone face back on. "What's up" she said.

"I was wondering if we could catch a cup of coffee and discuss the case."

She looked him up and down and said, "I need to shower but if you don't mind me as I am, we can go now."

Inside he cringed, dirty bitch. Won't even bother to clean herself up. This will be a pleasure. "We can take my car" he said, no need to take two.

"Ok" she said following him to his BMW. "Nice car" she said as he opened the door.

As she got in, she felt a prick on her arm. She looked up at him as she slumped into the car. She thought she saw the grim reaper. He buckled her in and closed her door. As he walked toward his door, Mr. Suit began to smile.

Evelyn woke up naked, strapped down on a table. Suit was sitting at a desk with his back to her. Without looking at her he said, "so you're finally awake. Or playing possum."

“Suit what in the hell are you doing?”

“What am I doing? That’s simple. I my dear are going to kill you.” He got up and walked over to a tray and brought it over to the table.

“Wait don’t do this. You don’t have to do this.”

“I do. I’ve always had to do this.”

It finally dawned on her. He was the killer. “It was you wasn’t it.”

“The woman wins a prize.

“What prize do I win” she said in a soft voice?

“I’ll kill you quickly!” He then reached toward her, she screamed and then there was nothing but silence.

Chapter 5

"Has anyone seen the D.A this morning? She usually beats me here." Someone in the bullpen yelled out, 'Maybe she got lucky last night.' Laughter broke out in the precinct. The chief just chuckled and walked into his office. It wasn't like she hid her sexual orientation. Maybe she did get lucky. Suit wasn't there yet either. The chief pondered the situation. Suit and the D.A? He thought to himself...Nah not even close.

Suit walked in right as he had the thought of them together. The chief quickly dismissed the thought from his head. "Jack, have you seen Gonzalez? She hasn't shown this morning."

Suit had a concerned look on his face as he spoke to the chief. "No, I haven't seen her. She is usually here when I get here. Maybe she is just running late. Have you called her cell phone?"

"No, I'm going to right now." The Chief called her cell phone. Her melodic voice answered, sending him straight to voice mail. The Chief left a message for her to call him and hung up.

"Anything"? Suit asked.

"No, went straight to voice mail. Well, she'll show eventually."

I walked in just as the chief finished his thought. "Who will show up later?" I asked as I walked into the office.

"Evelyn."

“What, she’s not here? That’s unusual. She gets here at the dawn of man.”

Suit looked at me and asked, “how do you know?”

“Eve, Evelyn has a sleeping disorder. It was nothing for her not to sleep for 2, 3 days. But then be out for another 2 to 3 days. I’ve been awakened more than once in the early morning because she wanted an update on a case. So, she may have just crashed out. Let’s just go on with what we have, and we will update her later.”

3 days later...

Friday morning, a patrolman walked into the chief's office and said, “excuse me chief, you may want to read this.”

“What is it?” The chief had a pale look on his face.

“They found Evelyn. Some patrons at the gym she goes to walked by her car in the parking lot and saw her slumped over in her seat. The police officers were called and after getting into the car found her with her throat slit. They are waiting for us at the scene.”

“Where’s Suit?”

“He got called back to Washington this morning.”

“Well, let’s go.” I wasn’t looking forward to this. Before this, other than the under-chief's daughter, the victims were unknown to us. He has changed the game. He’s made it personal.

Chapter 6

The coroner, Dr. Death as we called him, was waiting for us. He had a look on his that I could have sworn was that of unease. I've seen him at many a crime scene and he never showed any emotion. But now he looked extremely uncomfortable. Some might say he looked scared.

"Doc how's it hanging?" He tried and failed to bring a smile to his face.

"Stewart you're still an idiot.

"Yeah, and your point?"

"Wayne, she didn't deserve this."

"What doc?" All he could do was point at the body bag on the gurney. As I walked toward it, I heard the doc say "it's not pretty. It's downright disgusting."

As I opened the bag, the scent hit me first. I continued to open the bag and I couldn't help it. A cry escaped my lips. What I saw in the bag couldn't be Evelyn Gonzalez. But it was.

She had been skinned like an animal. All you could see was muscle. Her throat was slashed down to her spinal cord. I crossed myself and even though I haven't been a practicing catholic for years, I prayed she was dead before this all happened. Dr. Death was right, she didn't deserve this. Death spoke over my shoulder.

“She was dead before this happened. I won’t know COD until I get her on the table, but I’m willing to bet my medical degree she didn’t feel any of this.”

I zipped up the bag and said “get to it then” in a harsh voice. Harsher than I intended. Doc didn’t pay any attention to me and just said softly, “I’ll take good care of her.” He slid the gurney into his van and drove off.

The chief looked at me and asked, “is it that bad?”

“Worse” I said as I walked over to her car.

“We got to catch that son of a bitch. Quickly!” Suddenly the hairs on the back of my neck stood up. “He’s here,” I yelled, spread out.

Be careful he’s dangerous.” The chief yelled back, “you sure?”

“Real sure. Cocky bastard, aren’t you?”

Suit sat in the van looking out of his field glasses. Ok let’s have them run around like chickens for a bit. He sat back and thought of Evelyn Gonzalez’s final moments. I must say it was fun.

She laid on the cold steel table, spread eagled and strapped down. She knew she was going to die. Of that she was certain, she just wanted to know why. “So why are you killing young women? Did one do something to you? Couldn’t get it up?”

Suit whirled around and screamed “SHUT UP! You know nothing about her.”

“I know enough. She did a number on you. What happened? You can tell me. You have me who can I tell.” Suit calmed down and wiped the sweat from his brow. He began to speak, his voice trailing off in the distance.

"Her name was Joan, and she was the prettiest girl I had ever seen. Long blond hair with a body that would stop time. I was a shy kid and never spoke to anyone. I didn't have any friends, so I kept to myself. One day as I was walking down the hall, we bumped into each other. I apologized profusely. She said it's ok. Your name is Jack right.

I was surprised that she even knew who I was. After that day she went out of her way to either bump into or rub up against me. She had to know I was getting aroused. This went on for weeks, till one day she said would I walk her home? We walked to her house which was right around the corner from mine.

As we got to her house, she said would you come in for a minute. I have something to show you. We walked into her bedroom, and she said sit here. I'll be right back. I sat on her bed waiting for her to come out. She said softly here I come. She walked out of her bathroom. She was completely naked. She said I want you to make love to me. All I could do was stare at her naked body.

As I went to reach out and touch her, I ejaculated in my pants. She saw what I had done and laughed. She ran me out of her house laughing at me the whole time. I ran all the way home, crying the entire way. The next day when I saw her, she just started laughing. Her friends were laughing. The guys called me Quick Draw McGraw. I swore I would get my revenge. No one would laugh at me again."

Evelyn didn't say a word. She just listened. This guy was seriously unhinged. She took a big breath and asked. "What happened?"

Suit brought himself back and said, "one day after school I asked could I walk her home." She looked at me and said "why?"

"I got something to show you" I said with a smile on my face.

"Ok I'm game." As we walked to her house, I found a large rock that I had placed in a spot on the way to her house. She was talking and not paying attention to me. I got the rock and bashed her in the back of her head. I hit her repeatedly, until the rock was nothing but pebbles. Then I walked home. I burned the clothes in our fireplace and waited. I heard the sirens as they found her body. When they questioned me about walking her home, I lied and said she never showed up. At her funeral, I sat there and cried and cried. No one ever knew that I was the one that put her in that grave.

At this point, Evelyn decided to goad him into a rage. Hopefully, he would make a mistake. "Well don't talk about it anymore. It's boring. Come on do it." He looked at her, his rage building.

"Shut up! SHUT UP!!!"

"Come on Puta. DO IT!!" he cut her throat, and then began to stab her again and again.

Evelyn Gonzalez, the pride of her family. The first to graduate from college died drowning in her own blood.

Suit stood breathing hard looking at her on the table. He became mad at himself as he walked around the room. He let her take him out of his zone. He can't afford to let that happen again. It could be the difference between life and death.

His life or death.

Chapter 7

I was puzzled...who would take the county DA? And why? I knew that she had a lot of enemies and a quite a few of them would love to have killed her. But as we interviewed them, it was obvious that none of them had anything to do with her murder. Quite a few of them were surprised that she was dead.

I was also surprised that I had not heard from Suit. The chief said that he had not heard anything from him either. As much as he liked to be on top of things, his silence was unnerving.

I went to see Dr. Death to see if he had any other information for me. When I walked into the morgue, Doc was just sitting there. I could hear his silent sobbing, but I said nothing. Eventually he noticed that I was there. He made no attempt to hide his tear-stained face. “Wayne, you need to kill this son of a bitch. What he did to Evelyn was cruel and sadistic. No one should have to die that way.” I asked if she was alive during all of this. After a short pause, he looked me in the eyes and said one word,

“Yes.”

“She was stabbed and skinned. More than likely under the influence of a drug. I’ll know more when the tox screen comes back. No defensive wounds and no skin under the fingernails. Whoever killed her, she knew him.”

“I interviewed those who I thought might have wanted to kill her, but none of them had her on their radar.” Doc walked around the table and stared at her unclad body. He looked up at me and said, “Wayne kill the son of a bitch.”

As I went to walk out the door, I stopped and turned around. “Doc do me a favor. See if you can get any DNA. And run it through every data base we have.” “Including federal,” he said?

“Especially federal” I said over my shoulder as I walked out the door.

18 hours later...

Doc called me down to the inner sanctum as he calls his workspace. Dr. Strange indeed. “What’s up doc?”

“Chloroform was what knocked her out, but a drug nicknamed sux is what killed her.”

“Sux? Succinylcholine? Doesn’t that paralyze the muscles in the body?”

“Yes, and normally she would have suffocated, but with the damage her body had taken, her heart just stopped. Everything else was done postmortem. Wayne his rage is escalating. He has gone from very simple beating to skinning his victims alive. He must be put down like the rabid dog that he is.”

As I walked to the door doc said “you might want to sit for this. We were able to find a small spot of semen on her inner thigh. We ran the DNA through all the databases we had access to. And a few we didn’t. we got a damn match.”

“Who” I said?

“Mr. Suit.”

Just as I was going to say something, the chief ran into the morgue yelling at the top of his lungs. “Wayne, Doc lets go. There’s another victim.” As we ran out the door, I said “what’s the hurry”? The chief stopped and turned around and said,

“She’s alive.”

Chapter 8

“Wait she’s alive?”

“Yeah, but they don’t know if she is going to make it, so we got to go. Now!”

As we jumped into the chief’s cruiser, I let what had happened sink in. Suits DNA had come back in Gonzalez underwear. That wouldn’t bother me except she was a staunch lesbian and would not touch a man. I was perplexed about all of this. What in the hell was going on? And now he has left a victim alive? Something is wrong here. Definitely wrong.

Riverside Community Hospital

As we walked into the hospital, I stopped and said to the chief, “he is toying with us. He wanted us to get to her.” At that moment, my cell phone rang. I didn’t recognize the number, but I had a feeling I knew who it was.

“Mr. Suit, what can I do for you?”

“So, you did figure it out.”

“Yeah, I did.”

“Did you find the girl? Is she still alive?”

“Yeah, she is alive. You better hope she stays that way.”

“I don’t care if she does or not. You understand this is the endgame. I don’t plan on surviving this, and I plan on taking as many as I can with me. I suggest you get up there and talk to her. Don’t worry we will talk again”. He hung up before I could say anything else to him. Endgame he said. Indeed, it will be. His.

ICU

As I arrived the chief was speaking to the doctor. He looked at me and I said I would explain it to him later. The doctor said the young ladies name is Imani Williams. She is from Mobile Ala. She was at the Walgreens when she was attacked from behind. She is in a medically induced coma. She has a fractured skull. The chief said “I want 24-hour coverage at her room”. I told the chief I’d stay. With that I told him what suit told me.

“Do you think he will try for her here?”

“I’m sure of it: I said.

“Ok do what you need to do but don’t let anything happen to that young lady.”

“Trust me I said, it won’t”.

I walked over to her bed and stared down at her. This was someone’s daughter and mother. I promised to her that nothing would happen to her. Nothing.

2 hours later...

Suit walked into the hospital, his head on a swivel. He was wearing a white doctors lab coat. He took his time heading to the ICU, so he could see the defenses the police had set up. As he looked around, he thought about when he saw the young lady. He knew that Stewart wouldn’t be able to resist her. That would be his downfall. And hopefully his as well.

Stewart sat in his chair fading in and out. Vaguely he heard a voice outside her door. He slid into the bathroom as it gave him a good view to her bed. Someone in a white coat came into her room and looked around. They then they walked over to her bed. He picked up a pillow and started to cover her face with it. Stewart jumped out of the room and tackled him. They rolled around the room throwing punch after punch. Suit caught him with a kidney punch that took him down and ran out the door. Stewart wanted to give chase, but the pain was unbearable. The young lady was not hurt. Sleeping in her coma. I envy you young lady. I really do. The room door flew open, and the chief and two other police officers ran into the room.

"You ok," the chief asked as he looked around the room.

"Yeah, he caught me with a rather good body shot. How the hell did he get up here without being seen?"

"He killed a young doctor and took his credentials. He looked close enough, so the guard didn't question it. Neither did anyone else."

The chief glanced over to the bed. "How is she?"

Sleeping without a care in the world. The chief chuckled and told Stewart, "Go home and get some rest. I'll take the shift tonight". Stewart looked around and said be careful. He has tried once; nothing says he won't try again. Stewart walked out the door looking for a hot shower and a cold beer. And not necessarily in that order.

Suit sat in his apartment with an ice pack over his eye. Damn, Stewart packed a wallop in that right hand of his. I almost went down when he hit me. I got lucky with that kidney punch. I can't let him get that close to me again. Suit smiled; I took his measure. But he couldn't take mine. A voice in his head said don't get complacent. That's how we almost got caught last time. Yeah, but we didn't. Now to work on the next part of this operation.

Chapter 9

I walked into the chief's office after Evelyn's memorial. You couldn't call it a memorial; it was more like a party in a sense. There was a mariachi band playing and people telling stories that some of the people in the DA's and police department had never heard. Her partner, well her wife, something else they didn't know, told everyone stories about the other side of her. The kids she sponsored through school. The homeless that she helped to find homes and jobs. All in all, it was a very good day.

The chief walked in with a sheet of paper in his hand. "Wayne read this."

"What is it?"

"Suits last fitness report."

"I scanned through the report until I came to the end. In red and in big letters said, UNFIT FOR DUTY! "So, if he is unfit, how is he acting in an official capacity?"

"He isn't?"

I sat up in my chair "what do you mean he's not?"

"The FBI has been trying to catch him for years, but he always manages to give them the slip. They think this is their best chance to get him and they are sending a team in 48 hours."

"Wayne, you know if the FBI gets involved in this, we will never get him. He'll just go underground again."

"So, what do you want me to do?" I asked.

“Didn’t I hear you say you had a way to contact him? If so call him and do what you need to do you have 36 hours to get him. After that he belongs to the FBI.”

I looked at the chief and said “I’m too old for this.”

The chief smiled and said, “aren’t we all?”

As I turned and walked toward the door, the phone rang. “Hello. She is?” At my puzzled expression, the chief raised one finger. “Ok he will be right there.”

“Be right where?”

“The hospital. Imani is awake.”

“And she is asking for you.”

Riverside Community Hospital...

I took a good look around the hospital this time. I wasn’t up to anymore surprises. As I rode the elevator up, I wondered why she wanted to talk to me. I mean could it be she heard me as I talked to her while she was unconscious? I pondered that thought as I walked into her room.

She was talking with a nurse which gave me a chance to study her. Nice caramel completion, expressive face. Eyes a man could get used to staring into. Ok Stewart, down boy. I chuckled, and she looked at me and smiled.

Oh boy, what a smile. “Ms. Williams, welcome back to the land of the living.”

“It’s good to be back.”

The nurse looked at the 2 of us, laughed and said, “get a room you two, wait you’re in a room, carry on”. She giggled as she walked out of the room.

Imani said, “what was that all about?”

“I have no idea. Now Ms. Williams call me Mani” she said.

“Ok Mani, do you remember anything about the night you were attacked?”

“I remember going to Walgreens to get some allergy medicine. Then I walked to my car. I remember opening the door and then nothing.”

“According to the witnesses, after he hit you in the back of your head, he just walked off. Is this the man that hit you?” I showed her a picture of Suit.

“I don’t know but I remember him saying suit did it.”

“He told you that.”

“Yes, I do remember that.”

“Ok. Hold on a second.” I called the chief. “Chief come down to the hospital as soon as you can.” The voice I heard froze me in my tracks.

“I’m afraid the chief won’t be going anywhere for a while.”

“You son of a bitch, I swear if you’ve harmed him one iota.”

“Relax I haven’t harmed him. And if you do what I say he won’t be harmed. How’s the girl?”

“A headache and sore.”

"Good I didn't want to kill her. I needed her to draw you out."

"Me? Why me?"

"You were the only one who could do what I needed done."

"And what's that" I asked.

"Stop me."

2 days later, Stub Hub Center, 50-yard line 12 noon

I was there when he arrived. Suit wore a black jump suit. If looks could kill, I would be already dead. I wore a neon green wetsuit. Hopefully, this would absorb some of the blows.

Suit didn't say a word, just launched into a roundhouse kick that would have taken my head off if it had connected. I turned my shoulder into the blow and when it connected my shoulder went numb.

Great now I'm down to one good arm and two good legs. He sensed that I was in trouble and tried to grab me. This is where the wet suit came in handy. It was slippery enough to keep him from grabbing me. I grabbed him and was able to execute a long knee to the solar plexus. It took the air out him.

He charged and speared me to the ground. He commenced to hit me with right and left hands. My shoulder was coming back but wasn't fully recovered. I was starting to fade out when I heard her voice.

"Get up. Get up. Get him". Mani was here but why. Suit stopped for just one second. I was able to catch him in the throat with a short right hand. He rolled over and began to choke. I staggered to my feet and hit him in his throat again and again. I grabbed him by his head and just before I broke his neck I whispered in his ear, "you're done" and snapped his neck. As I fell to the ground, I heard Imani call my name. "hi", I said as I passed out.

Chapter 10

"Stop you how?"

"You see I've done this for so long, it's no longer a challenge. I want someone to stop me to put me out of my misery so to speak."

"So why me?"

"I've followed you. I saw how you put down that rogue twin brother of yours. You didn't even blink." Oh, I blinked but I wouldn't tell him.

"Ok so what do I have to do."

"Meet me in hand-to-hand combat at a place of my choosing. A fight to the death. No weapons. May the best man win." I thought about it for a second.

"Ok on one condition, that you let the chief go and if I lose, no harm will come to the girl." There was nothing but silence from the other end.

"Do we have a deal?"

"Deal!" came from the other end.

"Let me speak to the chief."

"Hello Wayne?"

"Yeah, Chief are you ok?"

"Yeah, I'm ok don't worry about me, put this ass hole down!"

"Got it chief."

"I'll call a car to come and get me."

"Ok put him back on the line,"

"Ok suit when and where."

"2 days from now. At 12 noon Stub Hub Center 50-yard line. Bring whomever you want. But the fight will be between the two of us. Agreed?"

"Agreed."

"See you in 2 days." The phone went silent.

I looked back at Imani. She had a look of concern on her face.

"You aren't going to do this are you?"

"Yes, I am."

"Why can't someone else do this?"

Epilogue

I woke up to a woman singing, in the hospital with some tightly wrapped ribs. What does a fellow have to do to get some peace and quiet around here?

Imani just looked at me and said "I ought to kill you myself. When you passed out, we rushed you to the emergency room. One ruptured spleen, and 3 broke ribs later they put you under, so you could heal."

"How long have I been out?"

"3 weeks!"

"And Suit?"

"Dead." was all that she said.

"So, I guess you're going back to Mobile now."

"Not if you don't want me too, I mean somebody's got to look out for you."

"Well, I do happen to have a secretary position open."

"No, you don't, I filled it."

"With whom" I asked as she walked towards the door.

She smiled over her shoulder and said, "Me."

WAYNE STEWART WILL RETURN

A Weeping Time

In Savannah Georgia in 1859

An act took place.

So heinous

It caused the heavens to cry.

The weeping time.

Over two days

On the plantation of Pierce Means Butler

437 men, women, and children

Were sold.

To satisfy gambling debts

Advertised in newspapers.

All over

It was determined.

To be a sale unlike any other

The text of some of the advertisements was, "For Sale, Long Cotton and Rice Negros! A gang of 440,

Accustomed to the culture of Rice and Provisions, among them are a no of good mechanics and house servants, will be sold on 2nd and 3rd day of March at Savannah by J Bryan."[7] It was advertised and announced from the beginning that there would be no division of families*

The two-day sale netted $303,850. The highest bid for a family, a mother and her five grown children, was for $6,180. Prices for an individual ranged from $250 to $1,750

Today 2 markers are all that's left
The largest slave sale in US history
Just to settle some debts
A weeping time indeed

*Slave Auction, 1859, Eyewitness to history

Underground Railroad

Come with me if you want to live.
Escape the chains of bondage.
To the north where we can be free
To live our lives as free men and women

This is no railroad of steel and rail.
The woods and swamps are the way we travel.
The dark of night is our friend.
Silence is the way we survive.

We will try to leave no one behind
But survival is up to you.
We will sacrifice no one.
But we will not sacrifice all just for one.

Take only what you can carry.
We move swiftly.
This is not a trip for the old or the maimed.
We flow as quickly as the mother Nile.

Come with me if you want to live.
Escape the chains of bondage.
To the north where we can be free
To live our lives as free men and women

The Traveler (epilogue)

I am the traveler. The last of a space faring race who traveled the galaxy. We have watched the development of species on thousands of worlds.

Unlike the watchers who refused to intervene, we would give a nudge to a race if we thought it was needed. One planet that we did this to was the one you call...

Earth

As I travel on this planet, I see all is not as we have planned. People are suffering. Some are unfairly treated. Some relish the thought of being in control. As the younger generation says, I am in my feelings about this.

I should intervene, but I will not. This is a problem that they must solve on their own. I will watch, but I will not interfere.

I know my time is coming to an end. But I cannot in good conscience not stay till I know that they will survive.

I am the traveler. But I believe that my travelling days are at an end. I will live here on this planet called earth. Until my end.

~~FINIS~~

Afterword

Have you ever watched something on the news or television in general and were so moved that you wanted to do something regarding what you just witnessed but just didn't know what? Have you ever wanted to tell a story but didn't know just what order to tell it?

If you have, then welcome to the unique writing styles of Mr. Anthony Arnold. A clever and unique storyteller, writer, and author.

Mr. Arnold is the type of writer that influences the reader to dig deeper after being presented with certain facts. This type of writing is different in its approach.

to the material presented because it forces the reader to continue the story that's been given and to find its end in their own terms to determine the outcome needed.

As once explained, Mr. Arnold stated to a reader "my job is not to tell you everything, my job is to light the fire so that you may want to find the rest on your own."

Being passionate about his people, and culture as part of his focus, and his writing in general helps guide this style as one would surmise while reading some of the other widely known authors in recent history.

Mr. Arnold speaks in the language of an eloquent scholar. It is that articulateness that comes across as the reader begins to turn the pages of the stories that have been written.

It is my hope that you enjoy this book in the spirit that it was written and gain some truthful insight into the world of one Anthony Arnold.

Warmly,

John L. Robinson, Jr. ~ Author

aka JRob ~ The Wise Son

About the Author

Anthony Arnold, born in Tampa, and raised by his grandmother in a small town called Quincy in the Florida panhandle, wrote his

first piece in the third grade and fell in love with writing ever since that moment; writing has become a comfort and a mainstay to keep him focused. As an avid reader of all genres of literature, Anthony has found a passion for black history.

He believes that his ancestry and the ones that have come before him have given their blood, sweat and tears to make it possible for him to live a life of freedom and liberation. Anthony is saddened to the fact that the current generation lacks knowledge and don't seem to know or speak of family history, our history or black history.

Writing gives Anthony the ability to educate those that have no clue about the things that African Americans have faced and write of things that they will never be taught in schools, shedding light on the strength of our people. Anthony's love for fellow man grew during his service to our country where he served and was awarded numerous medals, including The Air Force Achievement Medal-1986, 1993 and 2001 and many more.

His desire is to show the younger generation where they come from and to let them know we are much more than what society has labeled us! Winner of the 2015 National Poetry Awards Freedom Poet of the Year and the 2018 BHM Poet and the 2018 GANSPA people's choice For July. A 2022 UBAWA Black History Author and Holiday Month Author Feature.

Find more books and info about Anthony here.

Made in the USA
Monee, IL
17 July 2023